SEA QUEST

FANGOR
THE CRUNCHING GIANT

With special thanks to Tom Easton

For James Waldock

ORCHARD BOOKS

First published in Great Britain in 2016 by The Watts Publishing Group

1 3 5 7 9 10 8 6 4 2

Text © 2016 Beast Quest Limited.
Cover and inside illustrations by Artful Doodlers with special thanks to Bob and Justin
© Orchard Books 2016

Series created by Beast Quest Limited, London

A CIP catalogue record for this book is available from the British Library.

ISBN 978 1 40834 099 8

Printed and bound by CPI Group (UK) Ltd, Croydon, CR0 4YY

MIX
Paper from
responsible sources
FSC® C104740

The paper and board used in this book are made from wood from responsible sources

Orchard Books
An imprint of Hachette Children's Group
Part of The Watts Publishing Group Limited
Carmelite House, 50 Victoria Embankment, London EC4Y 0DZ

An Hachette UK Company
www.hachette.co.uk
www.hachettechildrens.co.uk

FANGOR
THE CRUNCHING GIANT

BY ADAM BLADE

ORCHARD

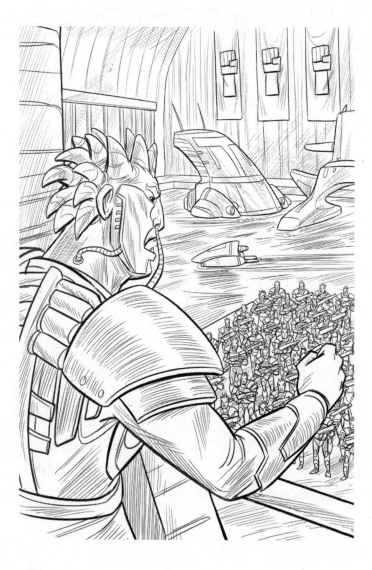

WAR IS COMING TO THE DELTA
QUADRANT!

For too long I have hidden in
exile, watching as Gustados, the
greatest of all civilisations,
becomes weak.

I have swum amongst the Merryn
of Sumara in disguise as one of
them, and stolen their secrets.
I have walked into Aquora,
Arctiria, Verdula and Gustados,
invisible to any around me. Now I
know how to destroy them.

Deception is the greatest weapon.
With it I will make the so-called
Delta Quadrant Alliance tear
itself apart! And in its place,
the Empire of Gustados will rise,
with me as its leader — Kade, the
Lord of Illusion!

CHAPTER ONE

BAD NEWS

"And so I'm afraid it looks like the Delta Quadrant Alliance may be on its last legs," Callum North said, his voice crackly with static. "I'm glad to hear you're safe, Max, just watch out for Ka—" A wave of static drowned him out, and Max punched the intercom button to respond.

"Dad, we're losing the signal. I'll try again when we're out of this trench."

"Goodbye, Max," Callum said, his voice full of concern. "And good luck."

"Goodbye, Dad," Max said. "And don't worry about Kade and his Robobeasts. Lia and I have that covered." Max swallowed as he signed off. The news from Aquora had not been good. War looked increasingly likely, and he couldn't help thinking, *Might that be the last time I ever speak to my dad?*

"Max sad," Rivet whined, then nuzzled his cold metal nose against Max's arm. Max forced a laugh and hugged his faithful dogbot.

"I'm okay, boy," Max said. Rivet barked, wagging his tail.

Max carried on with his inspection of the aquasphere's hull, checking every inch of the inside of the clear, orb-shaped vessel. He wanted to make sure it hadn't suffered significant damage during the recent fight with Gort the Deadly Snatcher. He shivered as he remembered the battle. The giant burrowing worm had crunched into the little sub more than once. Max knew that if the hull was damaged, the water pressure could squash the aquasphere like a bug on a windshield. Through the clear plexiglass of the sub's hull he saw his friend Lia glide by, riding her swordfish Spike. She still looked a bit pale after the injury she'd suffered when one of Gort's poison darts had struck her.

"Are you okay?" he asked her, through the communicator headset.

"That's the third time you've asked," she replied, with a tired smile. "I'm fine, and hungry enough to eat a kelp forest."

Max grinned. *She's back to herself, all right.* He decided it was time to take a break, and he and Lia ate a couple of seaweed cakes each.

Max looked up at the sheer sides of the Shadowreach canyon. The aquasphere was perched on a small ledge, near the bottom of

the trench. He'd been lucky to get a comms signal down here at all. There was just the faintest hint of sunlight and, apart from a few flitting fish and some hardy seaweed, he could see very little sealife.

"What's the news from your father?" Lia asked as they munched.

"I told him everything that's happened since we left Sumara," Max said. "Rescuing General Phero, discovering the four sleeping guardians in the Merryn temple and finally unmasking that shape-shifter Kade." *Our most dangerous enemy yet.*

"But how is the situation back home?" Lia asked, looking anxious. Max knew she was as worried as he was about the breakdown of the Delta Quadrant Alliance. Her own people, the Sumarans, would be caught up right in the middle of any war. Max shook his head sadly.

"Not good, I'm afraid," he said. "The members of the Delta Quadrant are at each other's throats. You and I know it was Kade who set off the bomb at the peace conference, but the Actirians are blaming the Gustadians, the Verdulans think the Aquorans are behind it, and the whole alliance looks like it's breaking apart."

"But Callum knows the truth," Lia said, puzzled. "Why doesn't he scramble the Aquoran battle fleet together and go after Kade?"

"He can't," Max explained. "The others would see it as an act of war."

"It sounds like there's going to be a war anyway," Lia pointed out.

"Not if we can help it there won't," Max said. He breathed in deeply. Determination surged through him at the thought of the task ahead. Despite the danger, he was raring to get going. "We have to stop Kade ourselves."

"I'm with you, Max," Lia said, her eyes flashing with anger. "That madman Kade stole my mother's ring. I'm not going to stop until the ring is back in Sumara, and Kade is in jail, where he belongs. Now, what's the plan?"

Max hesitated. He knew Lia was still weak from Gort's poison. He considered telling her to take it easy, but he knew that wouldn't go down too well. Her mother's ring wasn't just a precious jewel – Kade was using it to control the temple guardians: undersea beasts which he'd enhanced with deadly tech. They'd defeated Gort but there were still three more Robobeasts out there.

"We'll have to guess which way to go," Max said. "There's no way of knowing where Kade escaped to."

"Of course there is!" Lia said excitedly. "Think about it. Kade just wants to cause trouble amongst the alliance members. He doesn't care which, so he'll go to the closest."

"Which is?" Max asked.

"Verdula," Lia replied. Max knew his friend was the expert when it came to the oceans of Nemos. He looked up again at the featureless walls of the canyon. Down here in the darkness there were no landmarks, nothing to tell him which way was which. Lia spurred Spike on and zipped quickly around the aquasphere.

"We'll just travel along the Shadowreach," Lia went on. "It passes right by the island of the Verdulans. And, this way, we stay out of sight of any hostile forces from the other alliance members."

Max nodded and Rivet agreed. "Find Kade!" he barked.

Lia shot off along the trench floor on Spike's back, the swordfish's strong tail thrusting them along at a terrific rate. They were soon lost from sight in the murky water. "Come on, sea snail!" Max heard Lia cry.

Despite the peril to the Delta Quadrant, Max's heart pounded with excitement as he fired up the thrusters. The Quest was on!

He soon caught up with Lia and followed her closely. He saw Spike was staying tight to the bottom of the trench, weaving in and out of rocky outcrops and clumps of kelp. Max had to stay alert, tapping the steering column

lightly back and forth to avoid obstacles as the sub raced along the canyon floor.

"Keep your eye out for Kade's minions," Max said. But they saw no one, just shoals of darting fish and an occasional giant eel poking its grumpy face out of a sea cave. Max increased the power to the engines and felt himself thrill to the roar of the powerful thrusters, driving them along.

"Hot, Max," Rivet barked, after they'd been travelling for an hour or so. Max noticed he was sweating himself and flicked on the coolers.

"The sea's heating up," Lia confirmed over the intercom. "We're moving into tropical waters."

"Look," Max said, turning his head to watch a shoal of shimmering blue fish pass by. "The fish here are more colourful." He saw a school of parrotfish, then a few stub-nosed groupers carefully watching a small shark some distance away. A little more sunlight had begun to filter down through the water, suggesting they were in shallower seas. Max even saw the occasional patch of coral brightening the trench floor. Verdula was a tropical island. They must be getting closer. Max felt a shiver of anticipation. The last time he and Lia had been on the island they'd been attacked by a mutant crocodile.

Let's hope the reception this time is a little less toothy!

"What sort of fish is that?" he asked Lia, pointing at a large yellow and red fish approaching from ahead, slightly above them. Its colours were unnaturally vivid, almost as if they shone with their own light.

"I've no idea," Lia replied. "I've never seen one like it before." The strange fish seemed to be diving towards them. Cautious, Max slowed the aquasphere. *This doesn't feel right.* "Can you use your Aqua Powers to get it to change course?" he asked. "We don't want a collision."

"I'm trying," Lia replied nervously. "But it won't answer me."

Rivet barked and Max's heart skipped a beat as the fish's scales suddenly changed colour. Its glowing stripes flickered between yellow and red until the whole fish seemed to be a mad orange colour. On it came, quicker and quicker. *It's heading right for us,* Max thought.

Lia and Spike darted past the fish as it came fizzing towards the aquasphere like a shining torpedo. Spike swished his tail as he passed, creating a strong wave that knocked it off course. As it wobbled in the water Max gasped to see it shimmer with a kind of digital distortion, like a malfunctioning holo-screen.

For a moment the fish hologram blinked out
altogether, revealing the ugly truth beneath…
a streamlined metal tube covered with short
knobs – a device Max had seen before.

"That's not a fish," he said, his skin crawling
with fear. "It's a mine!"

CHAPTER TWO

SHOAL OF TERROR

Max yanked the steering lever into reverse and hit the thrusters. The aquasphere lurched back, just in time, as the mine-fish exploded right where they'd been. The shock wave sent them heaving forwards. Max felt his head crack against the console, leaving him dazed. He sat back in his seat and shook his head to clear it. He heard a hissing noise which he didn't like the sound of, but his first thought was for

Lia. Had she been caught in the blast?

But then he heard Lia speak over the intercom. "Are you okay, Max?" Max felt a wave of relief. "I'm okay, Lia." But the hissing noise grew louder. Max felt cold fear creep through him as he realised the sound was coming from the hull of the aquasphere itself. It was coated with some sticky substance which was even now trying to eat through the thick plexiglass. Max saw with horror that one of the sub's launchers had already been melted away.

Cloaked mine-fish filled with acidic goo? Max remembered the explosion back at the Sumaran peace conference. That had been a similar type of bomb. "There's no doubt about it," Max said. "This is the work of Kade."

"At least we know we're heading in the right direction now," Lia agreed.

"More fish, Max!" Rivet barked. Max spun

to see a spreading shoal of the colourful mine-fish swooping towards them. His heart leapt as he watched their bright stripes flick madly from red to yellow and back again. *The aquasphere can't take any more hits!* Again he hit the thrusters, steering left this time and down, as close to the coral as he dared. He turned to see Lia and Spike following closely. But his eyes widened as he saw the shoal speed up, bright orange now, just inches behind the frantically swimming Spike.

Homing mines!

Another of the mine-fish exploded and Max squinted against the bright flash. Half-blinded, he looked forwards again to see where they were going. Blinking to clear the after-image of the explosion from his vision, he dimly saw they were heading directly for a towering coral outcrop. Max wrenched the steering lever to the right. A wave of fear swept through him as he felt the aquasphere's left fin grind against the razor-sharp coral. *If the fin snaps, it'll be all over.*

Thankfully, the fin held and they sailed past the outcrop. The impact had knocked them off course, though. Max felt the aquasphere spin sluggishly in the water. He saw Lia behind,

still astride Spike, her face a mask of terror as a wall of mine-fish threatened to envelop her. A third mine-fish exploded and Max saw Lia duck to avoid the blast. "Lia in trouble, Max!" Rivet barked.

Thinking fast, Max hit the button to empty the ballast tanks. The aquasphere shot upwards like a cork and Max had to cling tightly to the steering column as he was thrown around. "Follow in the slipstream," he cried out to Lia. He saw her nod and slip in behind them as the aquasphere rocketed towards the surface. Risking a glance behind, Max saw that the mine-fish shoal was still following.

The canyon walls streaked past on either side. When they reached the top of the trench, Max levelled the aquasphere out and it streaked across the seabed, bright coral zipping past beneath the sub. Max turned quickly and saw with relief that Lia and Spike were still following, tucked in behind them. "Let's split up," he cried out. "It might confuse them." Lia and Spike darted right. Max yanked the aquasphere's steering column to the left and veered between two clumps of coral, hoping to shake his pursuers. Another blast went off behind and Max ducked instinctively.

Lia's voice crackled through the headset. "They're on your tail, Max!"

"How many?" he asked, braced for the next blast.

"All of them!" Lia cried. Max felt a trickle of sweat run down his back as he raced along at top speed, with a light flick here and there on the steering column to avoid a rock or a towering, jagged stand of coral. He noticed the water was getting shallower. Another blast went off, closer this time. The shoal was nearly on him.

The coral gave way to sand, sloping gently upwards. *A beach!* Racing along, Max had just enough time to yank back hard on the stick to avoid hitting the shelving ocean floor. The momentum carried them up, out of the water and into the air, breaching like an orca. Time seemed to slow as Max turned his head to see fountains of spray beneath them. A split second later he heard the dull thunder of multiple explosions as mine-fish after mine-fish rammed into the beach.

Rivet barked in alarm as the aquasphere twisted slightly and came crunching down into the sand. Max was thrown against the console with a thump and felt himself thrown back in his seat as the vessel rolled across the beach, once, twice, three times, before hitting something solid and coming to rest.

Max groaned as he sat up. "Ouch," barked Rivet. Max was distracted by a flashing light

on the console. It was next to a switch he hadn't paid much attention to before, but the display read LAND MODE'. Curious, Max flicked the switch and felt the aquasphere lurch to right itself, the fins retracting. *It works on land, too?* Still dizzy, Max opened the hatch and half-climbed, half-fell out onto the warm sand. He looked up to see Lia in the shallows, bobbing gently on Spike's back. She grinned at him.

"A flying submarine," she said. "Now I've really seen everything."

Max inspected their surroundings. The first thing he noticed was how hot it was. The white sand of the beach stretched as far as he could see in either direction. Shielding his eyes from the sun, he looked up and saw a dense wall of trees fringing the beach. Verdula, he remembered, was mostly flat and covered with rainforest. The jungle before them looked forbidding. Thick with vines and creepers, it was impossible to see more than a few feet within. Max could hear the calls and crashing of large animals and birds.

Lia told Spike to wait for her in an inlet a few dozen yards to their right and then she came ashore, splashing through the shallows.

"The aquasphere looks to be sound," Max said, checking the hull for cracks. "Hop in."

"Shouldn't we push it back into the water first?" Lia asked, confused.

"We're not travelling in the water," Max said. "We're travelling on land." Lia frowned, but got in, Rivet and Max following. Lia's long spear only just managed to fit in the cramped cabin. Lia and Max took seats and strapped themselves in. It was a squash in there with three of them. Rivet sat on Lia's lap, his front paws on the console. Max grabbed the steering column. He grinned in delight as the sub rolled forward on solid ground. It really was a marvel of technology – the outer hull spun like a rolling ball, but the cabin within ran on bearings and so stayed level. Max took a couple of turns on the beach to get used to the controls.

"You Breathers do come up with some strange ideas," Lia said, shaking her head, but Max thought he detected a faint hint of admiration in her voice.

Once he'd got the hang of it, Max took them down the beach until he found a gap in the trees wide enough to let the aquasphere through. It was a bumpy ride in the jungle, over rocks and fallen trees. "Careful, Max!" Lia said as they squeezed between two gnarled trees, trunks covered with strange creepers. Colourful birds watched them curiously. "It's bad enough being on land, without bouncing around in a giant ball."

"Better than walking," Max pointed out. "This is why I love technology so much. It makes life a lot easier. And fun!" he said, as

they went over the lip of a low, rocky ridge and dropped with a sickening lurch to the jungle floor. Rivet lost his balance as they landed and bashed his head into the console. "Headache, Max," he barked.

"Do you know where we're going?" Lia asked, clutching Rivet more tightly.

"I remember the island geography from the time we fought Tetrax the Swamp Crocodile," Max replied. "I'm navigating from memory."

"Great," Lia said. "All this amazing technology but you forgot to bring a map."

"We don't need a map," Max said. "We just need to find the river where we fought Tetrax." Max's skin prickled as he remembered the battle against the huge reptile. He still had nightmares about those hideous teeth.

"Well, I think we might have just found it," Lia said, pointing ahead. They had come to a raging torrent cutting through the jungle. Max felt a thrill as he sensed the thrumming vibrations of the water through the aquasphere's hull as it sat on the riverbank.

Max turned to Lia. "Are you ready?"

"Ready for what?" she asked.

"THIS!" Max said, and hit the thrusters. The aquasphere shot forward and dropped the few feet down into the water with a huge splash. Lia lost her grip on Rivet, who slid to the floor as Max fought for control. The current picked them up straight away and wrenched the aquasphere downstream. Max's breath was knocked out of him as the vessel slammed against hidden rocks. The steering column seemed to move itself back and forth as the rudder crunched against the rocky riverbed. Max saw that they were headed directly for a huge rock standing out of the white water. For a second he wondered if he'd made a terrible mistake driving into the rapids, before he suddenly gained control and hauled the steering column aside to avoid the collision.

Max swung the aquasphere back and forth as they negotiated the rapids. After a couple of minutes the worst of it was over and they found themselves in slightly calmer waters.

Lia turned to him, frowning. "Is that your idea of fun?" she asked.

Max's heart was pounding in his chest and his hands were shaking with the excitement of the rapids. "Yes," he said. "It is."

Lia shook her head. "We're here to find Kade. And so far there's no sign of him. Or the Verdulans. Maybe we've come to the wrong place after all." The aquasphere had arrived at a shallow, slow-moving section of river and Max drove them out of the water and up onto the bank, which was mostly clear of jungle. He wondered if someone had been clearing this path along the water's edge or if it was natural.

They drove over a smooth path of broken reeds, laid flat. "I'm not so sure we are in the wrong pla—"

His words were ripped from his throat as the bottom suddenly dropped out of the world and the aquasphere plunged sickeningly through the reeds into a pit below.

CHAPTER THREE

OLD FRIENDS?

The aquasphere thumped into mud at the bottom of the pit, thrusting Max and Lia forward in their seats. Max felt as though the seat belt was trying to crush the life out of him and he heard Lia gasping. Poor Rivet went clattering across the cockpit again, bouncing off the console panel and coming to rest against the windscreen. "Bash nose, Max."

Max released his seat belt with a groan and fell out of his seat. He inspected Rivet for damage, but the dogbot looked fine, if a little startled. Max gazed upwards through the plexiglass hull. He expected to see Kade's leering face looking down at them, but instead he saw at least a dozen furry heads with large, luminous eyes peering over the lip of the pit. He blinked to clear his blurry vision and saw familiar, tattooed faces. He sighed with relief.

"Verdulans," Lia said. "We're lucky it wasn't Kade."

"Agreed," replied Max. He opened the hatch and they clambered out. "Greetings," Max called up. "I am Max, of Aquora. This is Lia, of Sumara. We are friends of Verdula. Could you please help us out of this pit?"

The Verdulans jabbered and screamed back in their curious language. "YAARRGH! YAR-YAARRGH!" Max couldn't understand them, but the way they were shaking their spears worried him.

"I can use my Aqua Powers to communicate with them," Lia said. She placed two fingers on her temple and began to concentrate as the Verdulans carried on jabbering. One gestured with a long arm towards Max and Lia. Another raised her wooden spear and waved it angrily as she screeched. They seemed to be arguing amongst themselves, and Max felt his mouth grow dry with anticipation. "They're angry," Lia said. "They don't like visitors, and they've been told to be on their guard since the bomb went off at the Delta Quadrant Alliance conference. It nearly killed their elders."

"Tell them we're seeking the person responsible for that," Max suggested.

"I did," Lia said, frowning. She listened again. "They don't believe us. They think we're spies, or an advance party of an army coming to take their island from them. They're suggesting Sumara and Aquora are allying against them."

Max felt himself grow angry. "Maybe you could remind them of how we saved them from Tetrax?"

Lia closed her eyes and resumed her conversation with the Verdulans, but soon broke off. "They say they can't be sure it's us. They say all foreigners look the same to them."

"Watch out, Max!" Rivet barked. Max looked up just in time to see a spear flash past his face. It pinged off the hull of the aquasphere and buried itself in the side of the pit. "It looks like they've made a decision!" Max said. *The wrong one.*

Max and Lia dodged as more spears flew down at them. The Verdulans howled and jeered as they flung their weapons. Max, Lia and Rivet scuttled behind the aquasphere, which offered some protection at least. Breathing heavily, Max tried to collect his thoughts. How were they going to escape from the pit? Suddenly, Rivet barked as a spear hit his metal flank and bounced off, clattering harmlessly to the ground.

"That gives me an idea," said Max. He reached across to Rivet and rapidly adjusted the settings on the dogbot's rear leg boosters. "Hold on tight," he cried out to Lia, as yet another spear ricochetted off the aquasphere and zipped past his nose. Lia didn't need to be told twice. She took a firm grip around Rivet's neck. Max did the same.

"Now, Rivet!" he cried. Rivet leapt, using his super-powered thrusters. Max felt himself dragged like a rag-doll as Rivet shot up and out of the pit amidst a hail of spears. Letting go at just the right moment, Max fell lightly to the ground and rolled to get clear. He stood and turned, seeing Lia had done the same. They found themselves a dozen feet from the pit, dense jungle at their back and at least twenty-five howling Verdulan warriors facing them. Max's heart sank. *There are even more of them than I thought!*

The Verdulans wore loose clothes and most were adorned with jewellery made of bone or animal teeth. Each carried a short spear and some had knives, too. Max backed off as he watched the monkey-like creatures come hopping and leaping across the clearing, brandishing their spears. He drew his hyperblade and stood at the ready. Lia moved to stand beside him, holding her own spear. Max heard Rivet come crashing down into the forest some way off as the two sides faced off.

"Tell them we don't want to hurt them," Max said. "But we'll defend ourselves if necessary."

"I don't think they're in much of a mood to listen," Lia replied, as the Verdulans charged. Max parried the first spear blow, then a second. Seeing an opening, he slashed at one of the Verdulan warriors, cutting his arm and sending him howling off into the jungle. Immediately, though, two more sprang up to take his place. Lia fought skilfully, using her spear to defend herself against the thrusting attacks of the Verdulans, then knocking them aside with the butt.

Max's heart surged with hope when he saw Rivet come charging back through the jungle to join in the fight. The dogbot snapped a couple of spears with his super-strong jaws and hauled warriors away from the fight. But just as Max felt as though the Verdulans might retreat, he saw half a dozen of them swamp the dogbot and pull him to the ground. *I've got to help Rivet!* He watched in horror as one wrapped his muscular arms around Rivet's neck. With a fearsome wrench the creatures pulled Rivet's head from his body, leaving a trail of wires!

"No!" Max cried. Swinging his hyperblade wildly, he tried to clear a path through the battle to help his dogbot, but found himself beaten back by the Verdulan hordes.

"Ouch, Max," Rivet's head yelped as the monkey-warrior scuttled off towards the trees, cradling it. "Want body back...Max..." Rivet's voice faded as the Verdulan carrying the head dived into the jungle. Max stared, open-mouthed, in shock. *Rivet!*

"Max!" Lia cried, bringing his attention back to the battle. He turned to see the Verdulans had fallen back watchfully, leaving Rivet's body lying still in the mud. One of them jabbered at Lia, gesturing furiously and baring his large white teeth threateningly.

"He's saying we must throw down our weapons or we won't get the robot creature's head back." She hesitated. "Will Rivet be okay, Max?"

"He... He'll be fine," Max replied, breathing heavily, his mind racing furiously. "His head can control his body remotely. But if something happens to his head, then his memory banks will be wiped out. And his personality." He glanced over at his dogbot's body again with a sense of horror. *I can't lose Rivet!*

Lia threw her spear down at the lead Verdulan's feet. Max did the same with the hyperblade. "Careful with that," he said, as one of the warriors rushed forward to snatch it up. "It's sharp." More Verdulans scurried up to them, some carrying long ropes made from twisted vines. Max didn't resist as they wound the rope around him and soon found himself trussed tightly. He and Lia were tied to long poles and carried on the shoulders of their captors. Two monkey-like warriors ran ahead, with Rivet's body.

As Max and Lia were carried along behind, heading deeper into the jungle, more Verdulans appeared, screeching and jabbering at them from high branches.

Max fought his rising panic. He assumed they would be taken to the Verdulan city deep in the jungle. But what fate awaited them there, he could only guess…

CHAPTER FOUR

JUNGLE CITY

Occasionally, the warriors carrying Max and Lia passed the poles from which they hung onto the fresh shoulders of fellow Verdulans. The panic Max had felt slowly ebbed and was replaced by a sick dread as his mind kept imagining what might await them. They were completely helpless.

Eventually, they reached a bright clearing. Craning his neck, Max saw they had arrived at the Verdulan city and, despite the desperate situation, he was glad they'd finally got there.

Hopefully he'd be able to explain himself to the leaders and win their trust. *There must be someone here who will remember us?*

The city was mainly constructed of stone houses surrounding huge, towering pyramids of grey stone, covered in vines and twisting creepers. Here the river snaked past the city, slower and more sweeping than the raging torrent Max had tried to navigate

earlier. Max saw Verdulans stopping to watch them as they were paraded through.

As they travelled deeper into the city the river widened out into a shallow lagoon, its surface opaque with algae and some kind of choking weed. Max found himself puzzled by the appearance of the Verdulans. They seemed unhappy. Defeated. Max passed two females with small children and caught their

eye. The Verdulans stared back at him sadly.

They'd been brought to the base of the largest pyramid of all – the central, stepped monument at the very centre of the city. The great flight of stone steps led all the way up to the flat top. Their captors stopped and Max saw Lia brought up alongside him. Their eyes met and he tried to summon a reassuring smile.

"How are you feeling?" he whispered.

"Not great," Lia replied, hanging from the pole, her face flushed. She nodded towards the Verdulans who carried Rivet. "But at least my head's still attached to my body." The Verdulan carrying Rivet's head stood close by and Max smiled at his dogbot.

"Max alive!" Rivet barked at the sight of his master.

"You bet," Max said. "Don't worry, Rivet, we'll sort out this little…misunderstanding."

Standing on the lower steps of the pyramid Max saw an elderly Verdulan, somewhat taller than most. He wore a magnificent headdress, festooned with vibrantly coloured jungle flowers and bright feathers. His face was painted in red and white. "Finally," Max muttered to Lia. "Someone in charge."

One of their captors stepped forward and began chattering to the elder in what seemed like a respectful tone.

"What are they saying?" Max hissed to Lia.

"This is the shaman. The warrior is telling him we are spies," Lia replied. As she spoke, Max saw the shaman look over at them with great concern. Max caught his eye and saw anger within. More of the warriors brought forward the hyperblade, Lia's spear and Rivet's body, the hind legs twitching occasionally. They dropped these in front of the shaman for his inspection but he made a

curious sign with his long arms, and seemed to be scared of the objects.

Eventually, the shaman held up a gnarled hand to quieten the jabbering Verdulan warriors. Max realised this was his chance to explain. "I am Max, of Aquora, and—" But he was cut off as the shaman made another sign and Max felt the cold steel of a knife held against his throat by a Verdulan warrior.

The shaman seemed to be deep in thought.

A deathly quiet came over the assembled crowd. Max's mouth went dry and, as he swallowed, his neck brushed the sharp point of the knife. One word from the shaman and it would all be over.

"Scared, Max," Rivet's head whimpered.

Me, too.

The shaman seemed to reach a decision. He pointed at Max, then Lia, then Rivet and he began to speak in a deep sonorous tone. His voice grew in volume as he gradually became more animated.

"He agrees that we are spies," Lia muttered. "And he says our technology is evil."

The crowd was growing restless now, shouting and chanting. One warrior scuttled up to Max, brandishing her spear angrily. The guard who'd held his knife to Max's throat broke off to shove her away, but more Verdulans crowded around. Max strained, trying to break his bonds, but it was no use. The shaman's speech seemed to have reached a climax. The crowd howled and surged closer to their captives. Max found himself in the centre of a circle of spear points. Fear gripped him. *There's no escape!*

"Max!" Lia cried. "What do we do?" Max turned his head this way and that, desperately looking for a way out. Two Verdulan warriors glared angrily back at him and stepped forwards, pulling back their spears to strike. Max braced himself for the searing agony of the first thrust. But, suddenly, the two warriors were knocked aside by another Verdulan – one that Max recognised.

"Naybor!" Max cried, as relief flooded through him. *Just in time!*

Naybor was the chief of the Verdulans. Max and Lia had met him when they saved Verdula from Tetrax the Swamp Crocodile.

He was a good foot shorter than the shaman, and wore loose-fitting purple robes and a well-made necklace of shark's teeth. His large, glowing eyes blinked in surprise upon seeing Max, then he quickly shouted a command. The Verdulan crowd hesitated until Naybor repeated his order. The inner ring of Verdulans shuffled back a few steps. The shaman strode forward and said something to the chief.

"He wants to know what Naybor thinks he is doing," Lia said. Naybor began to speak, gesturing angrily. "Naybor is telling them how he was there at the Delta Quadrant Alliance peace conference. How you warned the delegates about the bomb." Max breathed slowly, trying to stay calm, wondering if he dared hope. Naybor was still talking and Lia translated again. "Now he's reminding them that we saved them from Tetrax. He's saying we are friends of Verdula."

Max could see some of the crowd nodding their heads. Two warriors stepped forward and slashed the vines securing Max and Lia to the poles. Max fell to the ground, stretching his aching back in relief. His hands were still bound, but at least things were looking up. Max watched as the shaman pointed to the weapons, and to Rivet's body, and jabbered angrily at Naybor.

"The shaman says he does not trust us," Lia said, stretching her long arms. "He's reminding them all about the dangers of technology."

Again Naybor spoke. Max began to feel he was winning the argument. He gave Lia a reassuring smile. She started to smile back, but then her expression turned to alarm as she looked past him, into the trees. Max turned to see the aquasphere. It was on the move!

Max stared in astonishment as the great sphere came crashing out of the jungle and raced towards them, with no one driving it! *Like it has a mind of its own...* The vehicle zoomed past the gathered Verdulans, and straight up the side of the great pyramid as the Verdulan crowd screamed in alarm, pointing. *How did it get out of the pit?* The aquasphere stopped halfway up the temple and turned, before launching itself off the side. Max watched in horror as the vessel came arcing down right into the middle of the crowd. Verdulans screeched and dived out of the way as the sub landed with a crash amongst them. It spun right around, stopped, and Max heard Lia cry out in alarm as it opened fire with its one undamaged blaster, sending the crowd running for cover.

Max didn't see any of the fleeing Verdulans hit directly, but a couple of nearby buildings were pulverised, stone chips flying like shrapnel and injuring those nearby. He saw Naybor helping Verdulans towards safety, but there was no sign of the shaman.

"Max," Lia cried. "What in all of Nemos is going on?"

Max had no answer. Could some defence

autopilot have been triggered when the aquasphere crashed into the pit? But his eyes narrowed as he saw the sub chasing down Verdulans and trying to crush them. That wasn't some simple defence protocol. *Someone is controlling the aquasphere!* The vessel raced across the clearing, firing again and again, blasting another building as the monkey-creatures raced back and forth in panic. "We have to stop it," Max said.

Lia ducked under a bolt of crackling energy from the aquasphere's gun. "Let's go," Max said, setting off towards the rogue sub, his hands still bound.

"I hope you have a good plan," Lia said, following.

"We'll find out," he panted. He ran up the steps of the pyramid, waited a few seconds for the aquasphere to come within range.

Swallowing his fear, Max leapt off.

CHAPTER FIVE

OUT OF CONTROL

Max landed on top of the aquasphere with a thump that knocked the wind out of him. Scrabbling and sliding, he just managed to hook his bound hands around the mounting of the firing blaster. The gun fired again and again, narrowly missing a huddled group of Verdulans, but taking out a small bamboo building with one blast.

"The plan?" Lia cried, as the aquasphere zoomed past her.

Before Max could reply, the aquasphere veered left, heading for a fleeing group of Verdulans who were carrying an injured female. Max felt himself thrown about by the sub's erratic weaving. Despite his purchase on the gun mounting, his body and legs were flipped around, threatening to throw him off. Max tried to break his bonds by tugging against the blaster but before he could do so, the aquasphere collided with something and bounced up high into the air. Max braced himself for the shock as they hit the ground.

CRUNCH! The aquasphere thumped into the muddy floor of the square, rattling Max's teeth before careening off to the right and ploughing into one of the low buildings, neatly demolishing a wall as it came to a stop. Max was flung through the air and landed on his back with a thud.

Winded, he struggled to get to his feet.

He peered across the square and saw that the thing they'd hit was Rivet's body, lying unnoticed in the mud. "Thanks, Rivet," he muttered. Then he groaned to see the aquasphere shift and start to move again. Ignoring his pain, he scrambled forwards and managed to open the hatch before the sub could pick up too much speed. Max dived in as the aquasphere shot off again. He looked around the cockpit. *What's controlling the vehicle?*

It took him a few seconds but then he saw it – a small metal chip with a blinking red light, attached to the control panel. *Some kind of bug.* The aquasphere lurched again and with a surge of alarm, Max realised that the sub was recalibrating the blaster. He looked to the targeting computer display and saw the crosshairs were locked on to a figure. *Lia!* She was helping an

injured Verdulan to his feet.

The blaster whined, powering up, readying its charge for a blast. Max lunged forwards and kicked the chip with his heel. It came off with a sharp snap and he tumbled backwards against the plexiglass. The aquasphere powered down immediately, and the blaster's barrel dipped as it went off-line.

The hatch opened and Lia poked her head

through. She grinned at Max. "Good old Rivet," she said. "Clever of him to leave his body right there." Then she disappeared.

Max groaned as his body protested. "I helped a bit," he muttered, stooping to retrieve the chip.

As Max clambered out of the hatch, the aquasphere was again surrounded by Verdulans, chattering angrily. Lia translated. "They say that since we brought the aquasphere, we are responsible for the damage it caused," she said, sighing. "They think we must have been controlling it remotely."

Max felt his stomach sink. After all they'd gone through, it seemed the Verdulans were turning against them again. The shaman reappeared, the crowd parting to let him through. He indicated Max and Lia then, without a word, pointed up at the great pyramid. A hushed muttering flowed across the crowd, striking dread into Max's heart. He felt hands grab him, and he and Lia were bundled across the plaza and up the steps, half carried, half dragged. Looking to his left he saw the shaman carrying Rivet's head as the dogbot barked furiously. "Let Max go!"

"The aquasphere was controlled by a chip," Max shouted when they reached the top. He tried to show them the device, which he still held in his hand. "We weren't controlling it. But someone was, and we need to find them." One of the guards snatched the chip from him, flung it to the ground and stamped on it, smashing it into pieces. Naybor appeared, pleading and wringing his hands, but the shaman ignored him. It was clear the Verdulan crowd was now firmly with the shaman.

Curse Kade, Max thought. *This* must *be his doing.* Lia was dragged up next to him and thrown to the ground with a cry of pain. Max counted the guards – four of them, plus the shaman. Naybor stood to one side, watching the proceedings helplessly.

Max's eyes were drawn to a cruel dagger hanging from the shaman's belt. *Is that for us?* Max looked around desperately, hoping to spy some way of escape. He could see the whole city laid out before him, with hundreds of Verdulans gathered at the foot of the pyramid, staring up, their hands protecting their eyes from the midday sun overhead. They seemed to be waiting for something. *An execution?* He saw the blue-green lagoon near the temple base. Beyond the city lay mile after mile of unbroken forest. Even if they could get away, and down the steps, they could never outrun the Verdulans. Silence fell as the shaman held out his arms, casting a long shadow down the steps. He began to speak.

"He says the Aquoran and Sumaran empires can no longer be trusted," Lia translated. "The Verdulans must send a message to the outsiders that the Delta Quadrant Alliance is ended, that Verdula will again be independent. He will show all of Nemos the righteousness of their cause in the eyes of the River God."

Down in the square, and as one, the Verdulan crowd turned its attention away from the temple, and towards the murky lagoon.

What river god? Max wondered.

The shaman walked over to Max and Lia. He knelt down, bringing his head close to Max's. Max could smell the heady scent of the flowers on his headdress and see his face paint cracking. "If you're going to leave your toys just lying about," the shaman said, in perfect

Aquoran, "you really should remember to lock them up." Max gasped in surprise as his captor carried on. "You never know just who's going to be wandering around using remote-control bugs to terrorise an island of furry primitives into mewling submission."

A fresh terror struck Max as realisation washed over him. *This is no shaman!* For a moment, his captor's bright eyes shimmered and in their place were the onyx eyes of a Gustadian.

Rivet's head barked furiously. "Kade, Max!"

Max saw Lia's mouth drop. She must have seen the holographic disguise slip, too.

Kade stood and stalked to the edge of the temple top once more. He shouted something in Verdulan. "*Fan-gor-shah!*" and the crowd below began to chant. A short phrase, repeated again and again. "*Fan-gor-*

shah! Fan-gor-shah! Fan-gor-shah!"

Max looked over at Lia, hoping for a translation. But his friend had gone deathly pale.

"What is it?" he hissed. "Lia, what does it mean?"

"Shah means god," Lia began. "Fangor is the name of this god. A river god, according to Kade."

Trying to stay calm, Max peered over the edge of the platform, down to the lagoon. The waters there were no longer still. As Max watched, heart in his mouth, he saw the pond weed swirl and shift as something huge rose from the depths. The crowd gasped as the shape emerged and the chanting stopped for a moment before resuming, louder than ever. Max saw a smooth, rounded back, covered with slimy weed and rotting vines. Then a massive, stubby head appeared, with a rounded snout and gigantic jaws which yawned wide, revealing stumpy, jagged teeth.

"It's a hippo," Lia breathed. "And it's

massive." The beast lumbered up out of the water, trailing muddy water behind itself. A foul stench rolled from the disturbed lagoon bed and the crowd of Verdulans scattered, giving the beast a wide berth.

Max saw a yellow stone attached to the hippo's forehead, glowing with an internal light. Max glanced over at Kade, still in disguise. His robe sleeve had fallen back and, on his finger, Max saw Lia's mother's ring glowing as well. This was no water god. It wasn't a real hippo either. *It's one of the temple guardians.*

"Isn't he beautiful?" Kade muttered to Max and Lia, too quietly for the Verdulan guards to hear. "Max, Lia, meet Fangor the Crunching Giant."

The beast lumbered towards the pyramid and looked up at Max and Lia. If there were robotics on the creature, they were hidden by the putrid lagoon weeds covering its body. Opening its great jaws, it roared hungrily.

Terror struck Max in the gut, like a steel fist. They were going to be swallowed whole.

CHAPTER SIX

REMOTE CONTROL

Kade lifted his arms and shouted something to the chanting crowd.

There must be a way out of this, Max thought furiously.

On the stones a few feet away, he saw the shattered remains of the chip that had controlled the aquasphere. *That's it!* Quickly, Max shuffled over to Lia, who looked pale with fear. "Cause a distraction," he muttered. Lia nodded at him bravely and took a deep breath. She stood, and before her guards could seize her again, stepped to the edge of the temple and shouted out to the crowd below. Though Max didn't understand what she was saying, he saw her pointing at Kade with her bound hands, and he guessed she was explaining their shaman wasn't who he appeared to be. But the chanting didn't stop. The Verdulans seemed too awestruck by the presence of their so-called river god.

Just as Max had hoped, the four guards all moved forward to take hold of Lia. The one who'd been carrying Rivet's head dropped it to leave his arms free, and Max felt a surge of hope. *That's a stroke of luck.* As the guards struggled with Lia, and Kade carried on with his chanting, Max found himself unattended for a moment. He shuffled to Rivet's head. He saw Naybor watching, but the chief did nothing to raise the alarm. When the dogbot's head saw his master, his eyes lit up, but Max held a finger to his lips before leaning forward and whispering instructions into Rivet's robotic ear.

"Got it, Max," Rivet yelped back. Max peered over the edge of the pyramid to see Fangor reaching the bottom of the steps, and beginning to climb. His huge bulk made for slow going. But Max could see immense power in those tree-stump legs, driving

the massive Robobeast upwards one step at a time, shaking the temple beneath it. Beyond Fangor, halfway across the square and forgotten by the chanting Verdulans, lay Rivet's body.

"Now, boy," Max whispered. As Max watched, the metal body twitched, then stood, spinning completely once, before running quickly towards the abandoned aquasphere on the far side of the square. Max made sure Rivet's head was facing his body, controlling it remotely as it went up onto its hind legs and fumbled with the catch. Max watched breathlessly. *Come on, boy, you can do it.*

Lia was still struggling against the guards who were trying to hold her down. Max grinned at Lia's performance. She'd already won them enough time… Down in the plaza he saw Rivet's body had released the lock, opened the hatch and clambered inside the aquasphere.

Kade strode over to Lia and grabbed her. "Be quiet, fish-girl," he snarled in Aquoran, before throwing her roughly down onto the smooth stones. Lia kicked him hard in the shin and he howled in pain. Max turned back to the aquasphere, which was moving forwards. Max could just make out Rivet's body inside, leaning on the steering lever. The vessel was picking up speed as it approached the pyramid. With a chorus of chattering wails, it scythed through the crowd, scattering Verdulans like bowling pins.

Fangor turned as it approached, roared and lunged at the approaching sub with its great jaws. But the aquasphere was too fast and swept by, clattering up the pyramid steps.

Max saw Kade's jaw drop as the aquasphere came bounding over the lip of the pyramid. The fake shaman was forced to drop flat as the sub sailed over his head, while the Verdulan guards panicked, diving aside. The aquasphere sped down the other side of the temple, as Rivet jumped out. Seeing his opportunity, Max held out his bound wrists.

"Quick, boy," he said to Rivet's head. "Get me out of these." Rivet's head opened his mouth and cut through the vines binding Max's wrists in one powerful chomp. But what Max saw when he looked up nearly made his heart stop. The stinking bulk of Fangor rose slowly into view over the top of the temple steps, its massive, rounded head smeared with swamp slime. Max's skin prickled as he saw one unblinking eye peering out of the matted and rotting pond scum.

Fangor hauled itself over the top step and stopped for a second to look around, before heading for Lia. The stone floor trembled with each thudding footfall. Lia tried to scramble away but Kade kicked her, sprawling, into the path of the massive Robobeast. The beast stank of rotting vegetation and foul swamp water. It opened its jaws, giving Max a close-up view of its hideous teeth. They seemed to be capped with sharp steel, gleaming wickedly in the harsh sun. *So it is a Robobeast!*

Max looked around for a weapon, but there was nothing. They had to get out of there. He threw the dogbot's head to Lia, who wasted no time in getting Rivet's jaws to bite through her bonds.

Fangor snapped at her as she fled with Rivet's head. *Time to go!* Max followed Lia down the steps on the far side of the temple, alongside Rivet's bounding body. He could see the aquasphere lying at the bottom, along with some other discarded objects.

"My hyperblade!" Max cried in delight as they reached the ground. He picked it up.

"And my spear," Lia added. "They must have been dropped by the guards as they fled."

A roar from behind told Max that Fangor hadn't given up the chase. They dived into the aquasphere and Max grabbed the controls, piloting them out through the stone houses and towards the jungle.

"How did Kade get the bug into the aquasphere?" Lia asked, as Max weaved rapidly between trees.

"I don't know," Max said. "I suspect he was watching us the whole time. As soon as the Verdulans left the pit, he must have retrieved the aquasphere and attached the bug." He looked at Lia. "Take the controls, there's something I need to do."

Lia frowned but took hold of the steering lever. "I don't like this," she said, as they crashed through the vegetation, crushing plants and sending birds shrieking in fear. "Look at all the damage we're doing to the jungle." But Max was too busy reattaching Rivet's head.

"Max," Lia said.

"There, good as new," Max said, as the

dogbot's head clicked into place.

Rivet barked joyfully.

"Max!" Lia repeated.

"What is it?" he replied.

"Look up!" Lia yelled. Max did so and jolted in surprise to see Verdulans, dozens of Verdulans, armed to the teeth and swinging through the branches. He was about to

tell Lia to speed up when he saw that the aquasphere was approaching a cliff edge. Lia was still looking up at the Verdulans! Max dived forward to grab the steering column but he was too late. They sailed out into thin air, twisting lazily and dropping faster and faster. Max saw Lia's hands slap down on the console as she tried to brace herself for the impact. He felt his stomach lurch wildly as the ground approached. Then…

CRUNCH!

The aquasphere landed heavily on sand and roll-bounced forward, out of control. Max's head smacked sharply against the hull. His vision blurred and bright flashes went off before his eyes. Then blackness overcame him.

○ ○ ○

"Max! Max!"

Max lifted his head and tried to focus.

Where am I?

"Max awake," barked Rivet.

"Get up, Max," Lia said. He blinked at her, then peered out through the plexiglass. *A beach.* In fact it was the same beach they'd left just a few hours ago. But this time it seemed to be swarming with Verdulan warriors, angrily waving spears.

"What happened?" he asked.

"We crashed," Lia said. "It was my fault, sorry."

"Never mind that. Are you okay?" Max asked.

"Yes, I'm fine," Lia replied. "You broke my fall. Sorry about that, too."

THUD! THUD!

Max leaped in alarm as a Verdulan warrior banged on the plexiglass hull with the butt of his spear. More joined in, until the thumping noise was deafening.

"Looks like we're trapped," Max said, rising to his feet. Through the glass he saw a taller figure approaching, wearing a brightly coloured headdress. He swallowed nervously. "And here comes Kade, still in disguise."

The relentless thundering of the Verdulan spears grew ever louder. Max felt his heart pound in response. He wondered briefly about using the blaster to take out Kade once and for all, but he realised he couldn't risk hurting any Verdulans – not if there was to be any chance at all of rebuilding the Delta Quadrant Alliance.

Kade tipped back his head and laughed in triumph.

CHAPTER SEVEN

SOMETHING IN THE WATER

Max took a deep breath to calm his nerves, then leaned down to open the hatch.

Lia's hand stopped him. "What are you doing?" she asked in astonishment. "You can't go out there!"

"I have no choice," Max said, unsheathing his hyperblade. "I've got to defeat Kade. Otherwise his meddling will cause an all-out war in the Delta Quadrant."

"And what if he defeats you?" Lia asked.

"Then at least I'll have tried," Max replied grimly. "Either way, the Quest will end here, and now."

"Then I'm coming with you," Lia said. "I'll hold the Verdulans off while you take on Kade."

Rivet barked. "Rivet too, Max!"

Max felt his heart swell with pride to know his friends were right behind him.

Quickly opening the hatch, Max dived out before the Verdulan warriors could move to stop him. He heard Lia and Rivet leap out behind him and then the sound of Lia's spear clashing with Verdulan weapons as she went on the attack.

Max darted towards Kade, knowing he might not have much time before the Verdulans overwhelmed Lia and Rivet. He slashed hard at his enemy, but Kade was ready

and parried the blow with his staff. Kade
followed quickly with a strike at Max's head
but Max swayed to the left, tripping Kade as
he came on. Max twisted and slashed again,
but Kade was quick. *How can I defeat him?*

As Kade strode towards Max, his staff at
the ready, Max saw his robe swing open

slightly, revealing a blinking control array on the Gustadian's belt. Max fended off a vicious sweep from his enemy, coming face-to-face with him. Though the shaman hologram was still in place, nothing could disguise those wicked, gleaming eyes just visible beneath the hologram. Suddenly, Max had an idea. He took a step back and waited for Kade to come at him. Again, Kade swung his weapon…but this time, instead of parrying the blow, Max dropped quickly to the ground and rolled under the staff. He heard it sizzle through the air, just missing his head.

Kade over-balanced and, as he stumbled, Max sprang to his feet, turned and hacked wildly. A little off-balance himself, he managed only to slice a gash in Kade's robes.

But a gash is all I need.

For an instant, Kade's disguise flickered and failed, revealing his true form beneath.

The hologram was restored in a flash, but not before the Verdulans had seen. *If Kade's stealth suit is damaged, the hologram fails.* The Verdulans who had been circling, waiting for their chance to bring Max down, stopped and pointed in astonishment at Kade, jabbering wildly to one another. The disguise flickered once more. Kade regained his feet, looking furious. He screamed at the Verdulans and pointed at Max, clearly wanting them to attack.

But the Verdulans hesitated, unsure who to trust. "Give up, Kade," Max said. "It's over for you." Relief flooded through him. He had won. Kade would be brought to justice and the alliance would be restored!

But Kade shook his head, a grin appearing on the face of his Verdulan disguise. Somehow his confidence gave Max a bad feeling. Kade reached into his robes and turned off the hologram, revealing himself in all his disfigured

glory, drawing gasps from the crowding
Verdulans. His skin was pale, and so thin that
knotted blue veins were visible beneath. Half
of his face was riddled with metal fragments
embedded in his skin, and Max shivered to
see the tube Kade used to breathe underwater
running out of his enemy's nostril and into a

hole in his neck. Kade wore moulded, black armour which Max knew included jet boots and hidden glue guns. Max could also see the Merryn ring on Kade's finger, and there on Kade's wrist was the special tech watch that enabled him to teleport short distances, and control his shape-shifting disguises. The Verdulans stared in fear and anger.

"You shouldn't have come here, Max," Kade said. "You should have left me alone."

"And why is that?" Max replied. *What else does Kade have up his sleeve?* "You've lost your allies now."

"I don't need these little monkeys," Kade said. "I have other friends."

Suddenly, the Verdulans screeched in alarm and pointed down the beach. Max felt a faint tremor underfoot and his stomach squirmed. Though reluctant to look away from his enemy, Max couldn't help himself.

He turned his head. Rising from the surf came the massive, heaving bulk of Fangor the Crunching Giant. The weeds and vines had been washed away by the seawater and Max gasped to see that the monster's hide was made of plated armour, covering the body and most of the head, leaving just one eye exposed.

"It must have swum all the way down the river to get here," Lia said, appearing beside Max. Fangor opened its mouth, revealing its metal-capped teeth. The Robobeast roared so loudly Max could feel the vibrations through the sand. The Verdulans turned and scampered away up the beach, disappearing into the dark jungle. But then Max noticed that not all of

them had run. Six stayed behind, and as one, they shimmered, transforming into tall, cruel-looking Gustadians. *Kade's minions!* They too were wearing stealth suits, just like Kade, as well as gleaming armour pads. Each carried a glue gun. They glared at Max and Lia with their icy-blue eyes.

"New plan needed, I think," Lia muttered.

"Okay. Err. How about you deal with the Gustadians?" Max said. "I'll take care of Fangor."

"Fine with me," Lia said quickly, eyeing the Robobeast, who was even now thundering up the beach, heading right for them. She darted off, Rivet at her side, and swung her spear at the first pair of Gustadians. They ducked and tumbled away.

Max shivered in fear as the ground shook beneath his feet. Fangor was moving at a surprising speed. He swallowed hard and wiped the sweat from his sword hand against his aquasuit.

Then he stepped forward and prepared to face Fangor.

CHAPTER EIGHT

BATTLE IS JOINED

*H*ow can I defeat an armoured giant?

Max knew the most important thing was to keep the raging Robobeast away from Lia and Rivet, who would be more than busy with the Gustadians and Kade. He darted to the left and ran across the hot sand, keeping one eye firmly on the giant hippo. Fangor changed direction and lumbered towards him, clearly intent on cutting him off. When he thought he'd gone far enough to ensure

Lia and Rivet were in no immediate danger, Max stopped and waited, mouth dry with terror, as the huge creature came closer and closer. The ground shook as the hippo's massive feet pounded into the beach. Once it got up speed, Fangor was quicker than it looked.

Max waited until Fangor was so close he could see his own reflection in the monster's eye. Then he dived to the right, slashing with the hyperblade as he did so. But the ultra-sharp blade just bounced off the Robobeast's thick armour with a clang. Max felt his arm throb as the force rebounded through the sword. To make matters worse, Fangor lashed out with a foot as it rushed past. *It's so fast!* The kick caught Max hard on the chest, knocking the wind out of him and leaving him gasping for air on the sand.

Max had thought his size and agility might

allow him to keep one step ahead. But now he could do nothing but lie on the sand, trying to get his breath back, while Fangor turned and lined up for another charge.

Coughing and gasping, Max forced himself to his feet and staggered towards the sea. *At least in there it can't trample me.* He glanced over at Lia and saw her still gamely fighting off Kade's minions. She was fighting at close quarters to make sure they couldn't use their deadly glue guns. Rivet had locked his jaws around Kade's arm and was dragging him across the sand, keeping him out of the fight. Max saw Kade crack his staff down on Rivet's back furiously, but to no avail.

Max dived into the sea and struck out into deep water, then turned to look for his attacker. The beast had followed him into the water and was powering after him. Max noticed the yellow stone set into the Robobeast's bulbous forehead, through which Kade was controlling it. *If only I could get my hands on that.*

Max swam hard to the left, hoping that Fangor would sweep past him, allowing him to clamber onto the Robobeast's broad back. But again Fangor seemed to guess Max's intentions and snapped its great mouth shut, generating a tidal wave which swamped Max and rolled him over, away from the hippo.

Heart pounding and lungs protesting, Max swam out further, trying to put some distance between himself and the monster. But still Fangor paddled, closer, closer, until Max felt the wake of the Robobeast pushing him under. He twisted in fear to see the great jaws opening, ready to chomp down on him, steel teeth glinting in the bright sunlight.

Just in time, Max arrowed down underneath the hippo, between its great forelegs. He headed for the bottom of the ocean, but Fangor dived down after him and, with a flick of its head, slammed its snout into Max's body and forced him up again, flipping him right out of the water. Max landed some distance away, belly-flopping untidily. He turned quickly in the water, breathing heavily. Fear gripping him, he waited for the hippo to reappear. But

it didn't. Instead, bubbles rose up around Max. He ducked under to look for his tormentor.

What he saw made him blink in astonishment. Fangor was running along the sandy bottom of the sea with its great thumping feet. When it was directly underneath Max it launched itself upwards, mouth gaping as wide as a sea-cave. *There's no escape!* Max braced for the crunch of the jaws.

But then a silver dart shot into view. *Spike!*

The swordfish rammed his long nose into the flank of the Robobeast, right between two plates of armour. Fangor exploded into a fury of thrashing, clouded by bubbles. It twisted and tried to snap at Spike.

Max drew his hyperblade and dived down, grabbing hold of the thrashing hippo's ear. The Robobeast roared, blasting more bubbles from its great lungs. It dropped to the bottom again, with a thump that nearly dislodged Max, then raced off across the ocean floor, towards the beach. Max clung on, repeatedly lifted up and slammed down against the armoured hide of the massive beast. Panic bubbled within his chest. He considered dropping the hyperblade so he could use both hands, but without it he'd be defenceless. Either way he was in trouble.

Max had been lucky so far, but if he fell off

CHAPTER NINE

THE FINAL STAND

Max clung on grimly as Fangor burst out of the water, sending a plume of salty spray high into the air. The lumbering Robobeast charged up the beach, sheets of water pouring from his armour plating. It was only a matter of time before Max lost his grip. With a last, desperate lunge, Max thrust the hyperblade forward and wedged the tip under the yellow stone. Seeming to sense what he was doing, Fangor gave a terrific leap and crashed down on the sand with its forefeet. The impact flipped Max over and threw him forward. He saw blue sky, green forest and, finally, yellow beach sail past his vision as he flew slowly through the air,

landing with a thump in the sand. Wincing with pain, he lifted his head and looked behind, sure the oncoming Robobeast would carry on and trample him.

But Fangor was standing still – completely still. Its mouth was slightly ajar, as if stopped in the process of preparing to roar. And then Max saw, lying in the sand a few feet away, the yellow stone. His hyperblade must have snapped it off just as he was thrown forward. *Fangor is no longer controlled by Kade!* Max watched in relief as the steel armour plates clunked and cracked and slid, one by one, from the hippo's back, thudding into the sand. The metal casings over the hippo's teeth also slipped off.

Max hauled himself to his feet and turned to see how Lia was getting on in the fight against Kade and his minions. He blinked in surprise to see the Gustadians neatly trussed up with vine-ropes, a dozen or so Verdulan warriors guarding them. And there was Lia, racing across the sand towards him, grinning from ear to ear.

"You did it, Max!" she cried. "You defeated Fangor!"

Max sheathed his hyperblade and they high-fived.

"Max safe!" barked Rivet, performing a quick back-flip of victory. The earth trembled gently and they turned to see Fangor trudging slowly back into the sea. "It's heading back to Deepholm Temple, to hibernate again," Lia said.

A splashing from the shallows made them look over to see Spike leaping gracefully through the air and waggling his fins before diving back under, causing hardly a ripple. "Thanks, Spike!" Max called. If it hadn't been for the swordfish he wouldn't have been standing there now.

"The Verdulans came back," Lia explained. "Naybor persuaded them to turn around and help us defeat the Gustadians."

"What about Kade?" Max asked, looking around for the evil trickster. Lia's face grew dark at the sound of their enemy's name.

"He escaped in the confusion," she said. "As soon as the fight turned against them."

"That's no surprise," Max said. "Without his Robobeasts, he's nothing but a coward." Max clenched his fists in frustration. Once more, Kade had slipped through their fingers. He straightened as Naybor approached. The Verdulan chief spoke in his strange, chattering tongue.

"He's thanking you for driving off that monstrous creature," Lia translated. "He also thanks you for unmasking the false shaman. He says your bravery is unsurpassed."

"Tell him he is welcome," Max said, nodding towards Naybor. "Please thank him for coming back to help defeat the Gustadians. And I'd like to thank his warriors too." But when Lia had translated this, Naybor held up a hand, stopping Max in his tracks. Naybor spoke again.

"He says it is better if you do not," Lia said, surprise in her voice. "He says we should

go now. Away from here!" Lia's voice grew angry as she translated this last sentence. "After all you have done for Verdula, you're being thrown off the island?" She seemed as if she were about to reply to Naybor when Max rested a hand on her arm.

"It's okay, Lia," he said. "I understand why. In these times no one trusts anyone, and we're not safe here."

Naybor spoke again. "He wishes they could hold a feast in your honour," Lia translated. "But, alas, his people will not accept it. But we should know this. To him, we will always be friends of Verdula." The Verdulan chief bowed gravely before turning and striding back towards his people, who were even now tying the Gustadians to poles, ready to carry them back to the city.

Max looked up at the trees lining the beach like a protective wall, closing off the island of Verdula from the rest of the world. In a way, Kade has succeeded, despite losing this battle. Unrest was growing in the Delta Quadrant, and former allies were growing apart, unable or unwilling to work together. War seemed closer than ever. The only thing that could prevent it would be capturing Kade and exposing his lies and his double-dealing. And that wasn't going to be easy, not when Kade still had two more terrifying Robobeasts left to do his bidding.

"So," Lia said, "what's the plan now?"

"The plan is we do whatever it takes to capture Kade and bring him to justice," Max said grimly. "It's down to us, Lia. You and me."

"Don't forget Spike," she said. "And Rivet, now he's back in one piece."

Rivet barked at the sound of his name. "If anyone can complete this quest," Max said, smiling, "it's the four of us."

THE END

FREE COLLECTOR CARDS INSIDE!

COLLECT ALL THE BOOKS
IN SEA QUEST SERIES 8:
THE LORD OF ILLUSION

978 1 40834 090 5

978 1 40834 099 8

978 1 40834 093 6

978 1 40834 095 0

OUT NOW!

Don't miss Max's next Sea Quest adventure,
when he faces

HYDROR
THE OCEAN HUNTER

WIN AN EXCLUSIVE GOODY BAG

In every Sea Quest book the Sea Quest logo is hidden in one of the pictures. Find the logo in this book, make a note of which page it appears on and go online to enter the competition at

www.seaquestbooks.co.uk

We will be picking five lucky winners to win some special Sea Quest goodies.

You can also send your entry on a postcard to:

Sea Quest Competition,
Orchard Books, Carmelite House
50 Victoria Embankment
London EC4Y 0DZ

Don't forget to include your name and address!

GOOD LUCK

Closing Date: 31st October 2016